Ella and Toy Rabbit

Story by Dawn McMillan

Illustrations by Pat Reynolds

Rigby®

A Harcourt Achieve Imprint

www.Rigby.com
1-800-531-5015

Ella and Grandma went into the toy shop.

"Look at the toys!" said Ella.

"I like this tiger,

and I like this horse!"

5

Grandma went to look at the puzzles.

Ella ran to look
at the toy rabbits.

"I like this baby rabbit,"
said Ella.
"Look at it, Grandma."

"**Grandma**," she cried,
"I cannot see you!"

8

Ella ran to look for Grandma.

"**Grandma**," she cried,
"where are you?"

10

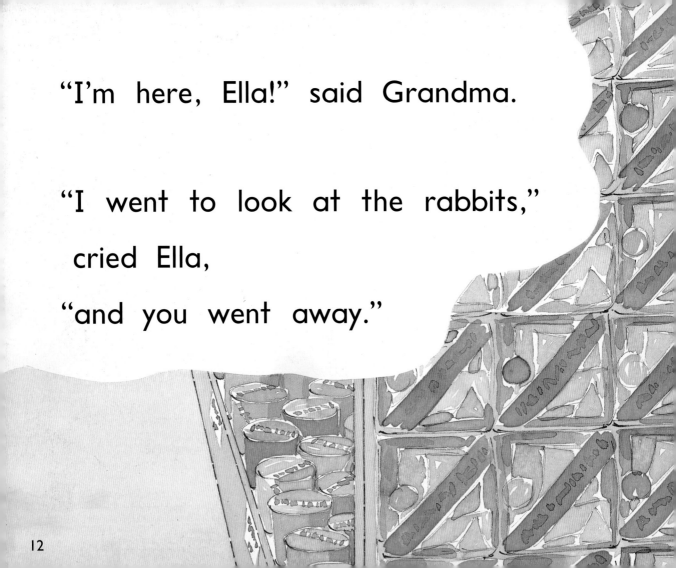

"I'm here, Ella!" said Grandma.

"I went to look at the rabbits,"
cried Ella,
"and you went away."

Grandma and Ella went back
to the toy rabbits.

"Here you are, Ella,"
said Grandma.

"I love this baby rabbit," said Ella.